THE POMS

A DOG-U-DRAMA

PART I

By Sylvia Pace
Illustrated by Elijah Taylor

Braughler™
Books
braughlerbooks.com

Jade and Casey lay leisurely on their dog bed down the hall from their owner's office at the corner of Rugby and Atlanta Avenues. They napped every day most of the day. Frequently, they woke up to observe Mr. Jamison walking down the hallway from his home office to get a drink out of the beverage cooler. Jade, a black 12 year old Shih Tzu Poodle mix, and Casey, a white, 15 year old Bichon Frisé, had lived as companions for the last eight years and had come to a sort of agreement about who was in charge.

It was definitely Jade and while she had lots of spunk, Casey was beginning to slow down. They were both rescues, but that's a story for another day.

Mr. Jamison had been working from home for six months now and they had adjusted to the intrusion upon their napping. They were used to Mrs. Jamison being home during the summer because she was a teacher. They also were used to the two boys, Elliott and Mason, being home during the summer. They were *not* used to Mr. Jamison being home though he would, on occasion, come over and rub them on the head. While Mrs. Jamison and the boys spoiled them, Mr. Jamison withheld their treats saying it, "wasn't good for them."

Jade was the yin to Casey's yang and had an internal clock that told her exactly when walking time was. Elliott was away in college and Mason, at the time of this story, had gone with his mother to get settled in at Duquesne University. Mr. Jamison was "batching" it or home alone.

At precisely 5:10 PM, Jade arose from her slumber and walked down the hall to get Mr. Jamison. She never had to do this with Mrs. Jamison because Mrs. Jamison was already trained. Mr. Jamison was proving very difficult to train despite using all of her tricks. Casey stayed in the dog bed. It took him a longer time to get up to walk and he cherished every additional bit of nap time he could get. Jade passed the kitchen, the foyer, the half-bath, the guest bedroom and the linen closet before reaching Mr. Jamison's office. Using her nose to nudge the door open, she walked in and went over to his leg. He was on the phone.

"Yes, Laura, we need to get those November reports out before we can do the year-end ones." Jade heard a muffled sound on the other end and then waited for the phone call to end. She then grabbed hold of Mr. Jamison's leg and began gently pulling. This was all quite beneath her and she was mildly irritated. The humans were supposed to all be trained by now and this one appeared to be a slow learner. Mr. Jamison looked down and snapped,

"I'll be with you in a minute. Go get Casey." Jade muttered a doggie "hmmff" and went back down the hall to get Casey.

Today, she was anxious for her walk. Today ...they were supposed to see the new dogs in the neighborhood that almost everyone in the dog world had been barking about. Jade was ready to go. The new dogs had moved two streets over and were considered to be quite a mystery. They were "twups (twin pups)" and there had never been any twups in their neighborhood before.

Jade trotted to Casey and barked in dog talk, "Casey get up..It's time to go walking and see the new dog twups. Mr. Jamison won't take us until you get up."

"Again?" asked Casey, still sitting with his eyes closed. "We just went walking this morning. Why are we walking again?" Jade was losing her patience....

"We go walking twice a day every day Casey and we have been doing it for 8 years...get up or I am going to nip your ears."

"I was just settling into my afternoon nap," said Casey. Jade glared at him and Casey slowly began to move. As he got up he said, "I am 15 years old and I don't need to be walked like I'm a pup."

Jade responded, "Well I am 12 years old and I do want my walk..and don't you want to meet the new twups? We haven't had new dog neighbors in quite some time. Casey was now standing up.

"I think the name, "Twups" is ridiculous," said Casey as he slowly sauntered behind Jade down the hallway. Jade headed toward the door and waited.

She heard Mr. Jamison leaving his office. Reaching her, he looked down and said, "I thought you were getting Casey."

"Hmmffff, really, these humans are too much," thought Jade as she turned around again to go get Casey. Casey was having one of his "spells" again in the hallway and had stopped. He was standing still and staring off into the distance.

Occasionally, she would catch him doing this. It was almost as if he was in a trance and she would have to bark and nip at his fur to get him to go. His extended dog family whispered that he had doggie dementia but Jade wasn't sure if it was that or stubbornness. "Casey!" she barked.

"Let's go!"

He slowly turned to look at her and said, "Ok, here I come," and began walking down the hallway toward the door.

"Moving kind of slow today, Casey?" asked Mr. Jamison. Casey just looked at him and thought, "I'm moving slowly everyday it seems. Getting old sure is hard."

The door opened and off they went. Well...sort of. Jade was always in front of Mr. Jamison and Casey was always well behind him. This forced Mr. Jamison to both look behind him and ahead of him which kept him continuously off balance on their walk. They turned left in front of the mailbox and headed toward Pierce Street.

As they crossed Pierce they ran into a Basenji named Ralph. They barked a greeting and then asked,

"Have you met the new dog neighbors...the twups?"

Ralph was a bit uppity, only attending the most exclusive doggie daycares, but he indulged them with a response, "Of course I have seen them, everyone has... and we've heard them too. I am not a fan." Ralph then turned his nose back up toward his owner and walked away.

A little further down they ran into their friend, Hopewell, a bull Mastiff who was big and burly, but as nice as a teddy bear. He did drool a lot so they stayed clear. He was across the street.

"Hopewell," they barked, "have you met the new dog neighbors?" Hopewell had a deep voice and he responded slowly..."Yessss, the twups you mean..."I've seen them but I haven't met them."

"Anything you can tell us about them?" they asked. Mr. Jamison was anxious to move on and did not understand what all of the incessant barking was about.

"Jade and Casey, keep walking, " he said as they continued barking. Annoyed, he sat and waited. Hopewell stopped walking and almost made his owner trip. He barked, "You might want to stay clear of them. I just have a feeling."

Jade was starting to fret. She had so hoped to meet some new nice dog neighbors and maybe have them over for a doggie play date. From what she was hearing, maybe this was not going to happen.

They finally reached Cambridge Avenue and rounded the corner. They waited for a car to pass by and then they began walking down the sidewalk toward the new home. Jade kept pulling ahead and Mr. Jamison had to tighten her leash. Casey was trodding along. They finally reached the new house.

Jade ran back and forth looking at the fenced back yard hoping to catch a glimpse. Casey stopped and stared.

Mr. Jamison had no idea what was going on and he scolded them,

"Let's go. We are just halfway done." Jade stood firm and that's just the time she saw movement.

At that exact moment, the sky dimmed, the air grew cooler and time stood stock still. She thought she heard eerie music in the background. Just as she thought she might have imagined the movement, the backyard of the new house started to rise, a bright light cut through the dimness and sparkles began to appear and fall everywhere.

The yard morphed into a hill and at the top of the hill staring down at them were...The Pomeranians.

They were absolutely beeyoutiful. Jade had never seen dogs like them before. They were identical with thick manicured white fur. Doggie diamonds hung from their collars and they were both carrying tiny dog purses. Their eyes sparkled but their mouths did not move. The yard started coming back down and Jade found herself face to face with them through the fence. Casey whispered, "They must be famous. Look at them." Jade looked through the fence and said, "Hi, my name is Jade and this is Casey." "The two responded, "We are known as, "The Poms." "The Poms," barked Jade. Short for "Pomeranians" of a most impressive breed. "But what are your names," barked Jade. Mr. Jamison was getting impatient. "We will tell you our names when the time is right, but right now we are simply, "The Poms."

Jade stared at them for a little while longer and then followed Mr. Jamison. When she got home, she sat on her dog bed and talked to Casey. "They were beautiful weren't they Casey?" "A tad snobbish if you ask me, and they wouldn't even give their real names." "I wonder why," asked Jade. "Well, obviously, they have something to hide, don't they?" barked Casey. "What do you think they have to hide?" barked Jade. "I don't know," barked Casey, "but they are definitely not who they appear to be.

Sylvia Pace was born in Oklahoma but now lives in a quaint Georgia town. Before she started writing, she picked up a degree in English Literature, a Master's Degree and was a teacher for almost 20 years. She has a wicked sense of humor and continues to use Times New Roman as her preferred font.

This book or any portion thereof may not be reproduced or used in any manner whatsoever without the express written permission of the publisher except for the use of brief quotations in a scholarly work or book review. For permissions or further information contact Braughler Books LLC at:
info@braughlerbooks.com

Illustrated by Elijah Taylor
Designed by Alexandra N. Segal

Printed in the United States of America

Published by Braughler Books LLC., Springboro, Ohio
ISBN: 978-1-955791-50-2

Library of Congress Control Number: 2022920909

Ordering information: Special discounts are available on quantity purchases by bookstores, corporations, associations, and others. For details, contact the publisher at: sales@braughlerbooks.com or at 937-58-BOOKS

For questions or comments about this book, please write to:
info@braughlerbooks.com

Braughler™
Books
braughlerbooks.com

CPSIA information can be obtained
at www.ICGtesting.com
Printed in the USA
BVHW092157100123
656048BV00001B/9